THE LOG CABIN CHRISTMAS

by Ellen Howard

illustrated by Ronald Himler

Holiday House / New York

Text copyright © 2000 by Ellen Howard
Illustrations copyright © 2000 by Ronald Himler, Inc.
ALL RIGHTS RESERVED
Printed in the United States of America
www.holidayhouse.com
First Edition

Text typeface is Goudy Old Style Bold.

The illustrations were created using
watercolor and gouache.

Library of Congress Cataloging-in-Publication Data
Howard, Ellen.
The log cabin Christmas / by Ellen Howard; illustrated by Ronald Himler.—1st ed.
p. cm.
Summary: Elvirey decides that her family really needs to celebrate Christmas
even though it will not be the same since her mother died.
ISBN 0-8234-1381-0
[1. Christmas Fiction. 2. Frontier and pioneer life—Michigan Fiction.
3. Family life—Michigan Fiction. 4. Michigan Fiction.]
I. Himler, Ronald, ill. II. Title.
PZ7.H83274Lp   2000
[E]—dc21   99-40855
CIP

For Layla Raine, from her granny
E. H.

To Karli Grace
R. H.

The snow had been a-snowing for days and days.

"We couldn't go to meetin' tomorrow, if there was a church," said Sis.

"Who wants to set in a cold old church?" said Bub. "There's better things to do on Christmas Day."

"What?" I cried. "What *will* we do?"

Sis and Bub was quiet. Bub shrugged and turned away.

"Take this here inside, Elvirey," Sis said, shoving a pail of snow at me. "Set it by the fire to melt."

"But…" I said.

"Git!" said Sis.

So I hauled in the snow for water, thinking on Christmas
back home. Back home, in Carolina, our stockings was hung
for St. Nick'las to fill. We had fruitcake for dinner and singing.

When Sis came in, I whispered in her ear. "We can still hang
our stockin's," I said. "We can have a fruitcake."

Sis shook her head.

"Elvirey, I reckon St. Nick'las ain't like to come, now that
Mam is gone," she said. "Christmas is tomorrow. It takes weeks
to age a cake."

I could hardly take it in. No church. No stockings. No stick
candy or toys. No fruitcake for Christmas dinner.

"Ain't there gonna be no Christmas?" I said.

Sis just hung her head.

Granny was nodding beside the fire. I ran to her chair
and tugged on her arm.

"Ain't there gonna be no Christmas, Granny?" I cried.

"Hush up, child," she said.

So I hushed my mouth, but my head kept right on talking. We
had to have a Christmas, I thought. Mam would have said so right
out. Mam would have *made* a Christmas. But Mam was dead.

I didn't say nothing when Pap and Bub came in. They stomped their feet and beat their arms to chase away the cold. Then they settled to mending harness whilst Sis and Granny sewed.

That was what we did these snowy days. It was too cold to do most outdoor work. Too cold for building. Too cold for washing. Too cold for traveling far.

"It's heathen," Granny said of a sudden, "to have no preachin' on Christmas Day."

"Come spring, we'll see about buildin' a church," Pap said.

"I doubt I'll live to see it."

"Well, there ain't no church for miles around," cried Pap. "There ain't no preachin' to go to!"

"I didn't fetch us to this godforsaken place," said Granny.

Pap jumped up, knocking over his stool.

"Git out from underfoot, Elvirey!" he hollered, stumbling over me. He stomped out of the cabin.

Granny sank back in her chair and rocked hard, muttering to the fire.

"Shove over," quarreled Bub, poking Sis in the ribs. "You're a-hoggin' the warm."

"Look who's a-talkin'," Sis said.

I made myself small in my corner. My tears wet the quilt I was piecing. I pondered on Christmas.

Mam had loved Christmas. She used to put ivy and holly in a jug on the table, holly on the mantel, and ivy above the door. She used to cook and bake 'til the house was fragrant with spice. She used to sing and hum the day long—"Joy to the World!" She used to set candles a-burning.

"You'll set the house afire," Granny would fuss, but I could tell she wasn't vexed.

"It's to light Mary and Joseph on their way," Mam would say. "It's to help them find the stable."

"You're a daft one," Pap would say, but he'd smile and pat her hand.

Sis and Bub would giggle, full of secrets....

We *needed* Christmas!

There wasn't no holly bush beside the cabin door here in Michigan. But there was pine trees galore. Pine is green like holly, I thought. It smells powerful fine.

So when the sun came out at midday, I tied my shawl over my head and borrowed Sis's coat.

"I'm goin' for a walk," I said, and no one said me nay.

"Don't go too far, Elvirey," Granny said.

"Don't git all wet," said Sis.

"Stay out o' trouble," said Bub.

The cold caught my breath and turned it to clouds. My cheeks got stiff and pained.

But I found some pine branches and cut them with my knife. Soon my arms was laden. I turned towards home, following the chimney smoke.

"Don't bring that truck in here," said Granny.

"It's for Christmas!" I said.

"Fool!" said Bub.

But Sis said to him, "Shet up!"

I stood on my stool to put pine on the door top and string it on the mantel. The puny sprigs went into Mam's china jug, and I set it on the table.

"Wish't we had holly berries," I said. I didn't heed Sis, a-rootin' in the quilt scrap sack.

Granny eased up from her rocker and commenced to stir up something.

Then Pap came in with a big tub of snow.

"We need washin' up," he said.

Being littlest, I was last to wash. By the time I was clean,
a shoofly pie was cooling on the table.

"For Christmas dinner," Granny said.

The cabin was spicy and steamy. The dark had crept up to the door. I saw there was bows of red in the pine boughs, from scraps that Sis had found. Bub fetched out the candles.

"You'll set the house afire," Granny fussed as he set them in the window, on the mantel and the table.

"It's to light Mary and Joseph on their way," I told her, and Sis said, "It's to help them find the stable."

"Foolishness," Granny muttered, but she set herself to rock.

One by one, the candles was lit.

"We're a-goin' to have Christmas," I said with a sigh.

"Bless you, child," said Granny, and Pap patted my hand.

Then we was peaceful, Granny and Pap and Sis and Bub and me…. Seemed like Mam was with us, too.

Creak, creak went Granny's chair. *Snap, pop* went the fire. We breathed in molasses and fresh pine smell and the warmth of candle smoke.

Of a sudden, I heard Granny's singing voice rise, quavery and thin, above the creak of her chair. Sis joined in, then Bub, then Pap. I looked at their faces, aglow in the light. Then I opened my mouth and sang.

"Joy to the World!"